Catch that Crocodile!
Copyright © 1999

For the text: Anushka Ravishankar
For the illustrations: Pulak Biswas

For this edition:
Tara Publishing Ltd., UK < www.tarabooks.com/uk >
and
Tara Publishing, India < www.tarabooks.com >

First printed 1999, this edition 2007

Design: Rathna Ramanathan, Minus9 Design
Production: C. Arumugam
Printed in Thailand by Sirivatana Interprint PCL.

ISBN 978-81-86211-63-2

Catch
that
Crocodile!

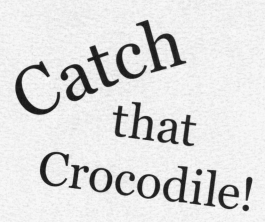

Anushka Ravishankar
Pulak Biswas

TARA PUBLISHING

Falguni Fruitseller sells fresh fruits

Banana!

Guava!

Mango!

she hoots

Come and buy a fresh papayaaaaaAAA

Wh...what!
H...how?
Wh...why?
Wh...which?

CROCODILE!

CROCODILE!

In the ditch!

Where did it come from?
How did it come?
The river is far
It couldn't have swum

Maybe it swam
With the floods into town
And got stuck in the mud
When the water went down

There's Probin Policeman
With a stick
Policeman, catch that crocodile!

Quick!

I'll give it a ticket
I'll charge it a fine
I'll put it in jail

- -

For crossing the line

I'll give it a bright
green signal to
GO

But catch that crocodile?

Me?

No, no, no

DO IT!

There's Doctor Dutta
What has he brought?
A measles injection?
A cholera shot?

I can tie up a python
In 7 small knots
I once cured a leopard
Of 62 spots

This crocodile needs
A strong sleeping dose
When it is asleep
I'll knot up its nose

But Doctor Dutta
Had spoken too soon
With a flick
The injection
Changed its direction

The doctor will wake up in June

Bhayanak Singh
The wrestler from Banaras!
He can catch
That crocodile for us!

Hayakilikile

ee

He leapt with a shout

The crocodile smiled
And opened its snout
Bhayanak Singh
Hopped quickly out

Is this the famous Man of Iron
Known to have elephants
Walk on his belly?

Is this the Hero
With biceps of rock?

Or is this a new brand
Of shivering jelly?

Meena walked by
With the fish she was selling
She stopped when she heard
All the bawling and yelling

Stay away!
It's a wicked reptile!

All I see is a lost crocodile.

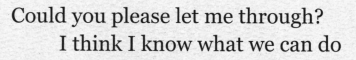

Could you please let me through?
I think I know what we can do

YOU?

One,

two,

three,

four...

Alright crocodile, off you go!

Meena's plan was really quite clever
The crocodile ate its way to the river!